Caroline Earle White

A holiday in Spain and Norway

Caroline Earle White

A holiday in Spain and Norway

ISBN/EAN: 9783743344907

Manufactured in Europe, USA, Canada, Australia, Japa

Cover: Foto ©Andreas Hilbeck / pixelio.de

Manufactured and distributed by brebook publishing software
(www.brebook.com)

Caroline Earle White

A holiday in Spain and Norway

A HOLIDAY
IN
SPAIN AND NORWAY

By

Caroline Earle White

Author of

"Love in the Tropics" and "A Modern Agrippa and
Patience Barker"

Philadelphia

J. B. Lippincott Company

Mdcccxcv

PRINTED BY J. B. LIPPINCOTT COMPANY, PHILADELPHIA, U.S.A.

PREFACE

THESE letters were written often in the hurry of rapid travel, when the writer was obliged at times to leave and return to them, her train of thought being broken, consequently they may appear somewhat discursive. They give, however, a correct picture of the countries which they describe, countries as yet rarely visited by the majority of American tourists, and hence may prove interesting.

C. E. W.

SPAIN

Dear ——.

At last we are in Spain, the country which we have so much desired to visit for several years,—sunny Spain, the land of romance and song, the scene of the long contest for supremacy between the Moors and the Christians, a struggle that has left its ineffaceable marks here, not only in the abandoned and desecrated works of art, but in its effect upon the character and customs of the people. We entered at Barcelona, the Liverpool of Spain, nearly two weeks ago, and spent several days there. It is the most prosperous city of the kingdom, and most resembles one of our American towns in the bustle and air of business which pervade the community, but in the attractions of great works of art, and the monuments of by-gone ages, it is behind all the rest of its sisters. It possesses an exceedingly fine opera house,

where one evening we attended the performance.   It was here that, last Novem-
ber, the bomb was thrown by one of the
anarchists which killed twenty-two people
and wounded more than fifty more.   In
seeing the spot where this occurrence took
place, and hearing the details, we realized
more than ever before the wickedness of
the species of warfare which consists in
killing and wounding innocent men and
women and children.   If anarchists wish
to advance their cause, and to lighten the
evils under which the working-classes
labor, they must choose some other means
than these.   It is said that ever since the
bomb was thrown in the opera house at
Barcelona many of the people, and the
aristocracy in particular, have refrained
from going there.   The evening that we
attended the performance there were
guards posted all around the building and
through the galleries.   On the first of
May there were six thousand soldiers collected in the city, in order to quell a dis-
turbance, provided any should occur ; but

everything passed off quietly. The annual
exhibition of paintings was open while we
were there, but, judging from most of the
pictures which we saw, we should say that
art is now in Spain at a very low ebb.
Wishing to continue our journey along
the eastern coast as far as there was any
railroad to permit of our doing so, we left
Barcelona in the morning and late in the
afternoon reached Tarragona. The Spanish trains go very slowly, and, when they
arrive at a place, do not seem to be in any
hurry to leave it. The mails go with each
train in a separate car marked "correos,"
and there is a box with a slit on the outside of each mail-car, called in Spanish
"buzon," in which at the different stations
people can deposit their letters as they
would in a post-office. The mails are
also distributed at each station; and we
were much amused, on one occasion,
while the train appeared to be waiting an
indefinite time with no one getting off or
getting on, at seeing one of the officials
reading aloud a letter to a peasant, who,

as we supposed, had just received it, and was unable to read or write. These immensely long stops at some of the trifling wayside stations, we have never been able to comprehend.

Tarragona is a curious old town, beautifully situated on a height overlooking the Mediterranean. The inhabitants are very poor, and the houses, of a Moorish or Eastern appearance, are unattractive in their exterior. The visits of strangers there must be like those of angels, "few and far between," judging from the manner in which we were received, for, when we went out to see the old cathedral in which was the tomb of Godfrey of Bouillon, we were soon followed by a crowd of children, going everywhere that we went, precisely as if we had been a travelling circus or menagerie. Finding such notoriety somewhat embarrassing, we soon concluded to return to the hotel, though not until we had carefully inspected the curiosities of the cathedral. One respect in which it differed from others we have seen

was that all its huge pillars were covered
with hangings of the finest tapestry, rep-
resenting sacred subjects, all embroidered
by the nuns of Tarragona. The next day
we left there for Valencia. The first part
of the long journey we skirted the coast
as we had done between Barcelona and
Tarragona, and had our eyes gladdened
by a constant view of the blue Mediterranean ; but after a time the railway struck
inland, and we were soon travelling through
groves of orange trees well-nigh as thick
as leaves in Vallombrosa. We had hitherto seen mostly olive trees and vineyards,
where the grape-vines were cut down to
the height of a little over a foot, together
with occasional fields of grain ; but as we
neared Valencia, we beheld little but orange
trees, most of them in blossom and some
bearing fruit. The air was redolent with
their fragrance, and we enjoyed to the
utmost our first experience of such travel.
We found Valencia, where we stayed a
couple of days, a city of considerable importance as a seaport, but otherwise pos-

sessing few attractions, although we were
told that the people were unusually social
and friendly. There, as in Barcelona, the
custom prevailed of driving flocks of goats
through the streets, and stopping them at
certain places in order to give their milk
to waiting customers. Each goat is provided with a bell hanging from a strap
around its neck, as well as a muzzle to
keep it from eating up all the tender plants
along the line of its march, to say nothing
of hand-bills and paper boxes. When it
rains, these valuable animals are provided
with an India-rubber, tightly-fitting blanket
or cover to prevent their taking cold.
They are milked out in the street anywhere apparently that any one comes up
with a pitcher or bowl desiring a supply
of the lacteal fluid. The tinkling of the
bells around their necks forms an important feature in the city noises every morning and evening, and is likely to disturb
the matutinal slumbers of those who
hear it for the first time. In Valencia, in
addition to the usual droves of goats,

cows appeared upon the scene, some of the inhabitants evidently preferring their milk to that of their smaller relatives. Whereas every goat was furnished with a small bell, every cow had a huge one around her neck, giving forth the most unmusical sound possible, and attached to her side, by means of straps or ropes, walked her latest offspring, in the shape of a young bull. All these little bulls were muzzled, but at stated intervals the muzzles were removed, and they were allowed to refresh themselves at the maternal fount. Every cow was invariably accompanied by her son, a custom, the reason for which we could not divine until it was suggested to us that cows have sometimes a habit of refusing to let down their milk until they know that a portion of it at least is to contribute to the nourishing of their offspring. All these curious sights in the heart of a great city interested us extremely, while at the same time our hearts were saddened with the reflection that all these little bovines were being reared for the purpose of affording a holiday amusement, by their tortures, suffering, and death in the bull-ring, to a cruel, excited crowd of spectators. Ice appears to be almost an unknown substance in Spain, and, as the weather at this time of the year is very warm, there arises the necessity not only of obtaining milk fresh at one's door, but of having a market every day in the week. The market square on Sunday in Valencia was the most busy and animated spot in the whole city, and many of the stalls were not closed till three or four o'clock in the afternoon. Meantime the churches were well filled, for a more devout nation than the Spaniards can hardly be found on the face of the globe. In the great cathedrals several masses are going on at the same time until ten or eleven o'clock every day in the week, and in the smaller churches there is at least one mass every hour. We heard a beautiful musical service on Sunday morning in Valencia. It appeared to be what is called the " Office of the

Blessed Virgin." Two fine male voices in the choir sang a portion of a hymn, and the congregation responded by singing the remainder, with the organ for an accompaniment. When we left Valencia, as we could no longer follow the sea-coast, the railroad not yet being built, we decided to go to Cordova. It was a long, uninteresting and tiresome journey, lasting nearly twenty-four hours. Travelling all night on a Spanish railway, even if in a first-class carriage, is not paradisiacal. We shudder to think of what it must be in a second-class conveyance. Soon after leaving Valencia, our eyes were greeted with an unusual sight, that of a large number of rice fields. They were all covered with water to the depth of two or three inches, recalling to our minds what we had heard of the unhealthfulness of rice cultivation. The country after a time became evidently less fertile, as we could see from the nature of the crops, and during the greater part of the day our road led through the arid and rather desolate province of La Man-

cha, famous for being the theatre of the
life and exploits of Cervantes' hero. The
land, being less rich than some of that
we had passed through, furnished a favorable soil for wild flowers, which grew in
profusion. We thought we had never
seen anything more beautiful than the
masses of the rich scarlet poppy inter-
spersed with a delicate blue flower re-
sembling a convolvulvus, which grew in
great quantities, and small yellow dande-
lions. The road-sides were a glory. Their
loveliness reconciled us to the absence of
the fertile, well-cultivated fields on which
we had gazed so long. We reached here
about eleven o'clock in the morning, and,
after taking our mid-day meal and an afternoon *siesta*, started out on a tour of in-
spection. Our steps were, of course, immediately directed towards the great
wonder of Cordova, the famous mosque,
now changed into a Catholic cathedral.
Though we had read of it all our lives,
we were unprepared for the marvellous
sight that burst upon our view as we en-

tered. It is of such immense dimensions
that it appeared to us even larger than
St. Peter's at Rome, and in whatever direction we turned our eyes we saw before
us a sea of arches supported by delicate,
slender pillars, yet in nothing like confusion, but arranged so symmetrically, that
wherever we turned there lengthened out
before us a wide vista with columns on
both sides stretching out almost inter-
minably. We were conducted by the
sexton to a portion of the edifice which
was to the Moslem the Holy of Holies,
and where the arabesques upon the arches
and walls were of the most superb de-
scription. Here there was an inner cir-
cular chamber with a fluted ceiling all cut
out of one piece of marble, surrounded
with inscriptions from the Koran engraved
in stone, the floor of which, although nearly
as hard as the solid rock, was worn in a
groove by the pilgrims to the mosque,
who used to walk around it seven times
in imitation of the ceremonies at Mecca.
This mosque was constructed purposely

with a view to its being used as a sacred shrine, and answering, instead of Mecca, as a spot to which the faithful might make an annual pilgrimage. This wonderful work of art was greatly impaired in the beauty of its interior by the Christians, who, when they gained possession of it in the fourteenth century, covered a large portion of the delicate arabesques on the walls with a thick coat of plaster. There is now being an attempt made to remove this plaster and restore the sacred edifice to its former condition.

GRENADA, May 12, 1894.

DEAR ——.

In all the places we have seen in Spain, none has pleased us so much as Cordova. Although the houses are of an Eastern simplicity externally, with bare white walls and little balconied windows, they are very attractive on account of their charming court-yards, generally filled with plants or flowers. Every house, except those of the very humblest order, is built with a square vestibule, having a brick or stone floor, and with heavy wooden outside doors that are kept wide open except at night. This vestibule leads into the court-yard with a gate between, the upper half of which is of open iron work, allowing passers-by to look through and see the flowers. Even the houses which have not the court-yard, have the little balconies outside the windows filled with geraniums, roses, and other flowering plants. The roses of Spain have been a wonder to us throughout our journey, and the same in Italy. Not only their beauty, but their cheapness is amazing to American minds. In Florence we could buy two or three dozen rose-buds in a bunch (and those of the finest varieties, such as we raise in hot houses at home) for six or eight cents. The cleanliness of Cordova is remarkable as well as the æsthetic taste of its inhabitants. We walked through its streets early in the morning, and everywhere they were being washed; not only the sidewalks, but the middle of the streets, the width of the whole being usually about twelve feet. There was the inevitable bull-ring in this as in all other towns of Spain, but we passed it by with as little notice as possible, to avoid the unpleasant suggestions caused by the sight. As we were leaving Cordova on our way here, we perceived some trouble in the railway carriage next to ours, and presently we heard some alarming screams. After a moment's reflection, we concluded that it must be an insane person who was being conveyed to a hospital, but upon inquiry we learned from the guard that it was a drunken woman. This surprised us greatly, as we had never seen an intoxicated man in Spain, much less a woman, but inquiring farther, we learned that it was an English woman. She was accompanied by one of her own countrymen with whom she was travelling, and she was evidently just getting over a spree. This occurrence caused something of a sensation, and a Spanish officer who was in our carriage entered into conversation with those of our party who could speak Spanish. He was from Cordova, and told us a great deal of the character and customs of the people of his native town. He said that their habits of thrift and cleanliness had descended to them from the Moors who so long inhabited Cordova, and that in many other respects they showed the influence of Moorish customs. The women, he said, were extremely modest and retiring, fond of seclusion, and preferring the company of their own to that of the opposite sex. Referring to the drunken woman in the neighboring carriage, he told us that in Cordova intoxication in females indicated the very extreme of degradation. No woman could sink lower than that. He mentioned, as an instance of the retiring habits of his towns-women, that a short time before he had gone on a little excursion with a small party of friends. There were some ladies among them, who enjoyed themselves very much until some strangers entered the railway carriage. They were gentlemen, but still they were strangers, and their presence made the ladies so uncomfortable that they insisted upon going into another carriage where they could be by themselves. We were passing at that time through a beautifully cultivated country with a long stretch of fertile fields on each side of the road. Our companion told us that it all belonged to the Duke of Medina Coeli, that as far as the eye could reach the land was his, and that he was enormously rich. We took the opportunity of asking him something we had long wished to know, —viz., whether the men who farmed the lands did it in shares, or in what manner they were paid for their work. He replied that they were compensated by a certain fixed sum, which never varied, so that they were sure of a maintenance in case the crops failed, or the taxes were increased. The farming, although very rude instruments were often used, that is, rude in comparison with ours at home, appeared to be remarkably well done, and we were told that this excellent method of cultivating the ground had also been taught to them by the Moors. There are often droughts of considerable length here and irrigation is very common. All the orange orchards that we have seen have been kept constantly moistened by artificial means, and, as I said before, the rice fields that we saw were covered with water to a depth of several inches. Until we came here to Grenada, we never saw a forest tree, unless we could consider as such a few scattered Lombardy poplars. Poor Spain has been denuded of almost all her forests. Orange and olive trees there are in great abundance, but they do not attain to any considerable height. After such a deprivation, it was all the more delightful to us to see the quantity of magnificent elms here at Grenada. Our hotel, the " Siete Suelos," looks right out upon the Alhambra. As we sit in the garden taking our morning coffee or our *déjeûner à la fourchette*, we are only separated by a wall from the historic pile. The roads in every direction around the Alhambra are bordered with these splendid trees, sent out here from England, and which cast so thick a shade that no other protection from the sun is necessary. The morning after our arrival we started at once, after taking our coffee, for the Alhambra. There is a large settlement of gypsies here, and we had not gone far before one of the women approached, begging to be allowed to tell our fortunes. We resisted her importunities for some time, but she was so attractive, with her black eyes and white teeth contrasting brilliantly with her dark skin, that at last we yielded, and allowed her to tell the fortune of an unmarried member of our party. The fortune, when it was told, was much in the style of such performances generally; but, after it was done, she proposed, if her payment was supplemented with another piece of silver, to tell us a fortunate number in the lottery. We declined, at the same time telling her that we did not approve of lotteries. This was

evidently a height of morality far beyond
her comprehension, and we left her in a
state of bewilderment. I do not propose
to say much of the Alhambra, since it is
the one thing in Spain with which Americans are particularly well acquainted. The
writings of Washington Irving have made
our country people feel at home here, if
nowhere else. We were conscious of a
little feeling of disappointment in seeing
it for the first time. It did not seem to
us so wonderful as the mosque at Cordova,
still, we thought many parts of it magnificent, particularly the Court of Lions and
the Hall of the Ambassadors. The grand
hall where Queen Isabella received Chris-
topher Columbus and promised him her
jewels to aid him in his undertaking—
when setting out for the journey which re-
sulted in the discovery of America—had
an especial interest for us, as well as the
smaller room with the fountain in the
middle where all the Abencerrages who
had incurred the displeasure of the Sul-
tan Boabdil were decapitated, their blood

mingling with the water of the fountain. There are many other places of ·interest here that we have visited,—the beautiful church dedicated to the famous Portuguese saint, St. John of God, and which contains his remains, the still handsomer Cartuja belonging to the monastery of the Carthusians, and the chapel of the Cathedral where are interred Ferdinand and Isabella, and their daughter Joanna, with her husband, Philip of Austria. A gentleman in our party descended into the vault and touched the coffins of the royal couples, but the effort being attended with considerable discomfort, the ladies did not attempt it. The sight of Joanna's effigy in marble recalled the sad story of the unfortunate queen, and we seemed to see before us the melancholy procession, continued during weeks of stormy and bitter weather, when she bore the body of her beautiful, intensely beloved husband from Austria to Spain, where it found a resting-place at last in the chapel where we beheld it. The loss of her consort, joined with her grief

at his indifference to her, when she loved
him so devotedly, bereft her of reason,
and, after the death of her father and
mother, she was kept in confinement for
many years by her son, Charles the Fifth,
never recovering her faculties so long as
she lived.   In the same chapel we were
shown the casket in which Queen Isabella
placed the jewels that were sold for the
benefit of Columbus, and some ecclesiasti-
cal vestments worn by Cardinal Mendoza,
as well as other objects of interest.   One
of the greatest pleasures that we have
had in connection with the Alhambra is
the ascent of the Torre de la Vela, and
the magnificent view we had from its summit, the beauty of which was greatly increased by the snow mountains of the
Sierra Nevada.   On one side lay all
Grenada at our feet, on the other the
great vega or plain stretched out before
us, with its fertile, well-cultivated fields,
and the river Genïl wandering along its
whole length.   The day was beautiful,
and the air as well as the prospect so

agreeable that we spent an hour or two
on top of the tower. We shall not soon
forget Grenada, with its Alhambra and its
gypsies and its groves of elms. It has
also some celebrated gardens, which we
have visited and found them most attractive, barring a little stiffness in the arrangement of the flower-beds and walks. Nowhere has the appearance of the people,
of the men especially, impressed us more
favorably than at Cordova. The officer
who was our travelling companion, said
that it was an unusually aristocratic city,
mentioning with considerable pride that
there were twenty-six noble families re-
siding within its walls. We were inclined
to believe there was something in what he
said, from the fact that one afternoon, while
we were in the great mosque or cathedral,
we had seen the funeral of a citizen who
held some public office, and we were impressed with the appearance of the men
attending it. One of them, whom we particularly noticed, had the head and face of
an Apollo. He was a man about fifty

years of age, with a perfectly Greek pro-
file, a figure worthy of his face, and a
high-bred air; at the same time modest
and quiet as if perfectly unconscious of
his attractions. Women do not attend fu-
nerals in Spain. There are peculiar customs in connection with their going to
church which it takes a stranger a little
while to learn. It is "de rigueur" to have
on a black dress and to wear a mantilla
when at mass. In the streets and at en-
tertainments we see them sometimes with
bonnets, but never in church. The younger
women take to bonnets kindly, but some
of the older ones refuse ever to wear
them. They evidently look upon them as
a corrupting influence, which, if not re-
pelled and kept at bay, may lead to a de-
terioration of morals. We have heard so
much of the Spanish mantilla and of its
picturesqueness, that we expected to find
it enhancing the good looks of its wearer,
but this is by no means the case. A pretty
bonnet or hat is in our opinion ten times
as becoming. Now we must start for

Gibraltar and Tangier, and say good-bye to you for the present.

TANGIER, MOROCCO, May 15, 1894.

DEAR ——,

Every American should come to Tangier, if he wishes to see the exact opposite of everything that he has ever beheld or known in all his life before. One can easily imagine upon arriving here that he is suddenly transplanted by a friendly genie and set down in the midst of a scene from the Arabian Nights. There is no road either in or around the city, consequently such a thing as a carriage is unknown. Everybody rides on a horse, a mule, or a donkey, unless he prefers Shanks's mare. The streets are all very narrow and paved with cobble stones, put down more unevenly than even those in the streets of Philadelphia, so that much exercise in the way of walking is not balsamic to the feet. Through these narrow streets, particularly the principal one of the town, pours a motley assemblage of Arabs, Moors, women in coarse, light cotton garments, with their faces covered up excepting the eyes, negroes, Jews, Europeans, and Americans, horses, mules, donkeys, camels, and dogs, all mixed up in inextricable confusion. Everybody walks in the middle of the street (there being, as a general thing, nowhere else to walk), and is consequently continually under the nose of a horse or a mule, or pushed aside by a donkey. Why we have not been run over before this when on foot, or why we have not run over somebody else when on a mule, is a standing marvel. Everything is so utterly and entirely different from all to which we have been accustomed that we were conscious of a feeling of surprise in seeing that the dogs and cats looked just like those at home. The houses are nearly all of plain whitewashed exteriors, two stories high, sometimes with pretty good sized windows on the second floor; sometimes with nothing but slits in the wall, only large

enough to allow the entrance of an in-
finitesmal quantity of light and air.   It
may be that these have open court-yards,
or are lighted in some other way ; as we
did not enter them, we cannot say.   We
have, however, gone into the lower story
of some that are very pretty, with large
halls and ornamented columns and ceil-
ings in the Moorish style of architecture.
A great many of the houses have shops
under them.   These shops are the most
curious places imaginable.   They are like
little booths, having no windows, and getting all their light from the open door-way.
There are no chairs in them, and the
Moors, who are their possessors, either
stand or squat, cross-legged, upon the
floor.   We entered one, to-day, larger
and of a more pretentious appearance.
In order to reach it we went into an entrance like that of a private house, then
through one or two hall-ways, and finally
out into the inevitable court-yard with a
tessellated marble floor and open to the
sky.   On one side of this court-yard was

the shop, on the others the living rooms of the family of the proprietor. He was a Jew from Tetuan, and was of a very sociable and friendly disposition. This was evinced, in the first place, by his making us acquainted with all his family, his wife at the head and a number of small children bringing up the rear. We were looking for embroideries, and we made a small purchase, not enough to have allowed any great amount of profit, so we must attribute it to his natural benevolence that, on the way out, he invited us to walk in and seat ourselves in what we suppose was his parlor. A music-box was then set going for our edification, and some refreshment was served to us in the shape of a kind of preserved fruit and glasses of cordial, the last emblematic, we thought, of the welcome we had received. We considered that, upon the whole, we could not have had better treatment even at the hands of a Christian. Yesterday we had our first mule ride in Tangier. Each mule was accompanied by an attendant in the shape of an Arab man or boy, and in addition we had a guide, who went with us on foot. We rode first through the main street of the town and out of the gate into the great market-place, which is always a scene of the most immense activity, tumult, and confusion. Here sit a line of women in the portion of the ground (for it is all on the bare ground and not in any enclosed or covered space) nearest to the wall of the town, selling vegetables and coal; beyond them an immense number of donkeys being loaded and unloaded; beyond them, again, droves of cattle, brought from the interior, to be sent away in boats to Gibraltar and Cadiz, and a little farther on, a quantity of camels just arrived from the desert, lying down to rest themselves after their long journey, in many cases the young ones lying at the side of their mothers. In the midst of this medley are men going around selling cakes and other eatables, musicians seated on the ground making a series of discordant sounds supposed to be attractive,

and which certainly attract a large crowd
to witness the performances of a snake-
charmer, and everywhere through it all,
beggars, beggars, beggars. The scene is
one that upon all occasions, or at least
when we have seen it, is simply indescribable. With the aid of our shouting at-
tendants, we made our way through it,
and were conducted to several places of
interest, the most remarkable among them
being that of the harem of the governor.
Only the ladies of our party were allowed
to enter here. We found five or six inmates, one being evidently a servant. Of
the others, the eldest was much the hand-
somest, but all had very fine eyes. They
were dressed in the Eastern costume, with
sashes very low down around their waists,
and some soft white stuff around their
heads. Their apartments consisted of
several rooms around an open court-yard,
all with beautifully tessellated floors in different colored stone. There was not a
chair anywhere, but low divans or couches
were spread around in the different rooms,

on which the women sat or reclined. They all sprang up as we entered and a lively conversation ensued, they speaking Arabic and we English. Neither party understood a word that the other said, so we did not make our visit a very long one. We then went to the prison, which is a woful place. We were allowed to look through a hole at the inmates, who were seated on the bare ground, in a wretched damp, dark, dirty place, making straw baskets. We gave a shilling to the guard seated at the door of the prison, although he did nothing for us, because we were told to do so by our guide; but we bought no baskets of the poor prisoners, which we regretted most sincerely afterwards, when we heard that the government, which confines them in such a terrible place, gives them nothing to eat, so that, were it not for the charity of visitors, they would starve to death. It is reported that such has been the fate of some of these miserable captives. The tales that we hear of the cruelty and tyranny of the government are almost incredible. An English lady, who has lived there for a number of years, told us that no Moor dares to have a handsome house exteriorly, or anything that would give rise to the suspicion that he has much money, as there would be, in such a case, some charge trumped up against him, and he would be thrown into prison and kept there until almost the last farthing had been squeezed out of him. For the same reason, an agriculturist has no incentive to any great effort in cultivating the ground, or raising anything extra in the way of crops, as it would at once be supposed that he was making money, and he would be pounced upon by the government. The poverty and dirt and squalor are indescribable, and yet, in spite of it all, there is a picturesqueness and air of romance and a glamour that can be found nowhere but in the East. After leaving the jail we rode onto a hill which gave us a fine view of the city, and then descended to the seashore, where the setting sun gilding the tops of some of the hills on the opposite side of the bay, and leaving others in shadow while it cast a rosy light on the softly lapping waves of the Mediterranean, made a picture which filled us with delight. We stopped in Gibraltar a couple of days before crossing over here. From Grenada we went to Algeciras, only a short distance from Gibraltar, on a new railroad lately finished. This portion of the road is in English hands, and is under the management of a Scotchman named Morrison. We met on the way a gentleman whose acquaintance we had made before in going from Tarragona to Certoza. He told us that he was travelling in Spain for the purpose of obtaining information with regard to the life and career of Pedro de Luna, a Spaniard, who was made Pope under the title of Benedict the Thirteenth, and afterwards declared schismatic by the Council of Constance. During the time that he occupied the Papal throne, he founded the University of St. Andrews in Scotland, and this gentleman, who was a

Scotchman, was endeavoring on behalf of the university to learn something more than has hitherto been known of its originator. On this journey to Algeciras, we had the finest scenery that we have been favored with anywhere in Spain. For some distance the mountains and ravines were quite as fine as anything we have seen in the Austrian Tyrol, and even suggested the magnificent journey over the St. Gothard pass. A few miles from Algeciras we came to some beautiful forests of cork trees. Their aspect was most refreshing, as we had seen no tall trees, except at Grenada, since entering Spain. These cork woods are a great place of resort for picnic parties from Gibraltar, and there was one in them at the time we arrived, waiting for our train to take them home. At Algeciras there is a pier built out into the sea, so that we could at once go on board the little steamer that was to take us over to Gibraltar. This pier, which is the only one to be found anywhere in that part of the Mediterranean,

is the result of the efforts of Mr. Morrison,
who, as we have said, is the manager of
the road. He told a friend of ours that,
for some months after the pier was built,
his life was in danger on account of the
indignation of the boatmen at having their
means of a livelihood interfered with.
Everywhere else, at Gibraltar, Tangier,
and Cadiz, we had to leave the steamer
and get out into little boats to be rowed
or sailed ashore. It is most annoying and
even dangerous when there is a strong
wind and the surf is high. At Tangier
the passengers have frequently to be carried ashore on the backs of slaves. It
seemed to us very surprising that the
British government, which has done so
much at Gibraltar and done it so well,
building fortifications and a sea-wall of so
magnificent a character, should have no
pier, and consequently subject all visitors
to such inconveniences. Gibraltar pleases
us very much, as it had done on a previous visit. Although we did not have the
curious sight which greeted us before, of

little donkeys a few days old being carried about in panniers on the backs of their mothers, we saw much else that was interesting. The Sunday afternoon that we were there we had one of the finest ocean drives that has ever fallen to our lot. It was to Europa Point, which juts out into the sea close to a high rock rising precipitously from the waves to the height of between one and two hundred feet. It seemed strange to us to get back to pounds, shillings, and pence, after having had pesetas and reals so long; but we had only just become accustomed to the English money, when we came over here where there is such a mixture that it is difficult to find out what you owe for anything. Sometimes it is shillings, sometimes pesetas, sometimes francs, and then there is a currency peculiar to Morocco, of which we do not even know the name. On the way over from Gibraltar, we noticed in the boat two youths of a brown complexion, dressed handsomely in the Moorish costume, who we judged were persons of some distinction. The sequel proved that we were correct, for after awhile our Scotch friend, who was very familiar with everything relating to Morocco, having spent much time there, recognized them as the sons of the Shereef of Wasan. In a short time their mother appeared, and our friend, who was acquainted with her, presented all our party to her. She was a white woman from England, who had gone to Morocco to take the position of governess in a family of note, and there had made the acquaintance of the aforesaid native prince, the Shereef of Wasan, who proposed to her to become one of his wives. She consented, thinking, no doubt, that the position of the wife of a noble Moor, even if one among many, was preferable to that of a poor governess. We were not of the same way of thinking, but it was she who had to make the choice, not we. When we landed at Tangier, the arrival of the two elegantly apparelled youths caused a great sensation, and, although the rain was falling heavily, they were followed by

a crowd as they made their way through
the streets on foot, of course, as there
seemed to be no other means of locomo-
tion practicable, to their abode. We
hoped that we might be able to enter a
mosque here, but we find that it is not
allowed. We have heard, however, the
call at sunset from the priest, followed by
a chorus of voices, "There is no God but
Allah, and Mahomet is His prophet!"
Even the animals in the streets seem to
partake of some of the curious habits of
the people. The dogs lie down flat in the
road, right in the way of donkeys, horses,
mules, and all the passers-by, and go
sound asleep, so sound that they look as
if they were dead. If a dog in our country should do such a thing, we should
think he had softening of the brain. The
donkeys, too, poor, ill-used creatures, are
so familiar with the human race that, as
Cowper says, "their tameness is shocking
to view." One day, when I was going
down a slight incline in the street, on
the uncomfortable cobble-stones, I felt

something with a rather heavy foot stepping on my dress behind me. As the garment in question was not very long, I thought how unpleasantly near some man must be to me, and turned around to remonstrate, when, behold, it was a donkey. We must quit, however, this interesting place, with its delightful climate and its many contradictions of pleasure and discomfort, and go to Cadiz in order to complete our Spanish tour.

SEVILLE, May 23, 1894.

DEAR ——.

This is one of the most interesting cities of Spain, and we have found so much to see, beside being very comfortable in an unusually nice hotel, that we have been here nearly a week, and do not intend to leave until after the celebration of the festival of Corpus Christi, which takes place to-morrow. We have been told that nowhere in Spain, indeed, nowhere in the whole world, is Corpus Christi cele-

brated as it is here. There is a wonderfully
curious ceremony, which is to be seen nowhere but here—a dance by the young men
and boys of the choir, which is to take
place after mass, and when this is over
there is to be a grand procession through
the principal streets of the city. Strangers
are staying over to-morrow to witness the
unusual spectacle, and seats in balconies
and windows along the route of the procession are bringing a high price. Awnings
are being put up to protect those march-
ing underneath from the sun,—or rain, in
case the weather should not be propitious,
—and the whole city is beginning to put
on an air of animation and excitement. I
am sorry to say that the ceremonies, or
shall I say festivities, of the day, are to be
terminated by a bull-fight in the afternoon.
Not only here, but in Grenada, and I do
not know how many other places, there
are to be bull-fights, or, as the Spaniards
call them, " corridas de toros," to-morrow
afternoon. The following notice that I
have copied is one that is posted up at the

entrance to our hotel where everybody can read it :

"The first grand bull-fight in Grenada [first of the season, it means] will take place on the 24th of May, Corpus Christi, when six fine bulls, bred by Señor D. Eduardo Miuro, of Seville, will be killed, the matadors being the celebrated swordsmen, Mazzantini and Lagartijillo.

"The second grand bull-fight follows on Sunday, 27th of May, when six fine bulls, bred by Señor D. José Orozeo, will be killed, the matadors being the famous swordsmen, Guarrita and Bombita."

An American acquaintance of ours passing along one of the principal streets lately saw a crowd collected, and, going up to find out what was the matter, saw posted up the head of a bull, killed in a "corrida" lately, which had been bred by the Duke of Veragua (the guest of the United States, last summer), and which had performed such wonders in killing three horses outright that his head had been preserved for exhibition. The Pope

has just been dealing a blow at this cher-
ished institution of the Spaniards, but it
will endure many blows, we imagine, before
it succumbs, it is so deeply rooted in the
affections of the Spanish people. It is
almost inconceivable that any amusement
involving such horrible cruelty should be
so popular with a people who seem, as a
general thing, kind and gentle, but so it
is. We are very glad, however, to have
met with several Spaniards who object to
it strongly, and have made a gesture of
repulsion when asked if they were going
to the bull-fight to-morrow. "God
never leaves himself without a witness in
any people or nation," so we are told in
Holy Writ. We came all the way from
Tangier to Cadiz by steamboat, and a
more uncomfortable journey we hope
never to have to take again. It occupied
about five hours, and we were all more or
less sea-sick. The Mediterranean is beautiful to look at, but very unpleasant to
sail on. There appears to be always, even
when it is the most quiet, a slight swell,

very favorable to "mal de mer." We
noticed it at Tangier when we went out
in a row-boat on the bay, on a lovely evening with very little wind.

Upon arriving in Cadiz, we had to leave
the steamer and be taken to the shore in
a small sail-boat, and then to pass the cus-
tom-house. We thought for once that we
would try a purely Spanish hotel, as all
of those that we have patronized hereto-
fore have been more or less French in
their style of cooking and in their general
management. We were very glad that we
did so, as it was an experience we liked
to have once, if not oftener, so we went
to the "Cuatro Naciónes." Nearly all
the dishes at the *déjeûner* and dinner had
garlic in them. It spoiled the fish for us,
but we liked the salad, in which there was
a plentiful supply, better than any we have
had. Some of the streets here have very
curious names. Our hotel in Cadiz was
in Isabella la Católica, and we have noticed
others that seem strange to us, such as
Angel de Sevadra, Reyes Católicos, Fer-

nan Caballero, and the one we are in here is Mendez Nuñez. Most of the streets are so narrow in all the cities of Spain, except perhaps Madrid, that two carriages cannot pass each other, so that certain ones are marked "Entrada de carruajes" (entrance for carriages), and others, "Salida de carruajes" (exit for carriages). On the way from Cadiz here in the train, we saw the immense salt works, which begin just after leaving that city. Large square or quadrangular basins are built, into which the sea-water is introduced and left to stand for some time, when the salt is obtained by evaporation. Great masses of it in a pyramidal shape stood at the side of the road, some of them so immense as to suggest the pyramid of Cheops. Salt is here, as in Italy, a government monopoly, and there are shops for the sale of salt and tobacco alone. The country here, in the southwest of Spain, is less attractive than that we have seen before. We noticed one novelty in the shape of hedges of the aloe or century plant, varied occasionally by a variety of the cactus, which grows to a considerable height, and has immense leaves with yellow blossoms growing out of the leaves, as in all the cactus family. These, with a date palm here and there, made the vegetation assume quite a tropical appearance. Cadiz is a pretty, neat-looking city, with few attractions in the way of sight-seeing. Here it is different. One of the most noted of the places of interest in Seville is the Alcazar, a Moorish palace in the style of the Alhambra, and even more beautiful we thought, although not so picturesquely situated. It is right in the heart of the city, close to the great cathedral. The Hall of Ambassadors is superb, and another very beautiful room is that in which one of the Spanish infantas was born. Very fine and extensive gardens partially surround the building, of which a number of the walks are so arranged that, when the water is turned on, fountain-like sprays are thrown up into the air from little holes at even distances all along the pavement, cooling the air and laying any dust that may have settled there. The cathedral is very fine, but we could not see it to advantage, as it is in process of repair on account of the destruction caused by the earthquake six years ago. Several of the immense pillars were so much injured that a considerable portion of the ceiling fell in, and it is a work of years to replace it. It is in this cathedral, in one of the chapels, that we found the celebrated picture, by Murillo, of St. Anthony of Padua, in which the figure of St. Anthony was cut out several years ago by a man who concealed himself in the church, and carried to New York and there exposed for sale. The theft was discovered and the portion of the picture that was taken returned here, and has been most skilfully restored to its original place. The bell-tower of the cathedral, called the Giralda, is one of the most beautiful in the world. On the top, acting as a weather-cock by pointing toward the direction in which the wind blows, is a figure of Faith, so skilfully constructed that it turns with the lightest breeze, although it weighs between two and three thousand pounds. The ascent of the Giralda is not made by steps, but by a gradual incline, so it is not at all fatiguing to go to the top. When there, a fine view can be obtained of the city and surrounding country ; but it is vastly inferior to that from the Torre de Vela in Grenada, there being no mountains to diversify the scene. In the Museum here are a number of fine paintings by Murillo, who was born in Seville, and to whom his native city does honor in various ways. There is a fine statue of him in front of the Museum. One of the curiosities of Seville is a house purporting to be an exact copy of that of Pontius Pilate in Jerusalem. We were told that it was precisely like it, and we entered full of faith ; but when we saw a building covered with Moorish ornamentation, we began to doubt, and the climax of our incredulity was reached when we were shown an inlaid table that we were assured was the exact counterpart of that on which the thirty pieces of silver were laid down when they were paid to Judas Iscariot. From that moment we were ready to leave, voting in our own minds the whole thing a farce. Much more interesting and worthy of consideration we found the ruins of the Colosseum at Italica, a few miles from Seville. They are remarkably well preserved and much in the style of the Roman Colosseum. We were shown the dens under ground where the lions and tigers were kept, and the openings through which they dashed into the amphitheatre, the room where the gladiators prepared themselves for contest, and another which purported to be that where the Christians, who were to be thrown to the wild beasts, were confined. The Roman emperors are said to have been born at Italica, and what surprised us still more was to learn that Pontius Pilate was a Spaniard. This did not prevent his being a Roman subject, as he was born in that part of Spain which at that time belonged to Rome.

We went, one day, to the great tobacco factory of Seville. It gives occupation to six thousand women and girls, although some of them, we are told, are very poorly paid. Many of them are mothers, and take their babies or young children with them to the factory. When walking through the different rooms and watching the operation of making the cigars and cigarettes, we saw numerous little ones lying asleep at the side of their mothers. Some of the girls make as high as four thousand cigarettes in a day. Of course we had Carmen in our minds from the time we entered the building until we left it. It was in Seville that the tobacco factory, in which she is represented in the opera to have worked, was situated. A few of the girls that we saw were pretty, the majority not at all so. We think that Mark Twain, when he described in his "Innocents Abroad" the women of Seville as so beautiful, must have drawn largely on his imagination. The Spanish women generally, that we have seen, have not

impressed us in the way of looks. They
have very little expression or play of
feature, and that little they lessen by
covering their faces with powder. The
prettiest girl we have met since entering
Spain is our chambermaid at this hotel,
who rejoices in the name of Pepa and who
does not powder. That custom appears
to be confined mostly to women of the
higher classes.

The Hotel de Madrid, where we are
staying, is said to be the best in all Spain.
It certainly is the best that we have seen.
It is patronized by the Princess Eulalia
and her husband, Don Antonio, the son
of the Duke of Montpensier, when they
come here in the winter to visit the
Dowager Duchess of Montpensier, who
lives in a fine palace near the river. The
principal drive of Seville is past this palace
and then along the bank of the Guadal-
quivir. We were there yesterday, and
were surprised to see among the eques-
trians so many little boys. We saw one
on a pony's back who did not look over

four or five years old, and a number only on spirited horses which they managed admirably. When we leave here for Madrid, we must start at six o'clock in the evening, and spend all night in the car. It is one of the unpleasing peculiarities of travel in Spain that nearly all the express trains leave at night, and, "nolens volens," one is obliged to take them when going a considerable distance, as, if one of the day trains should be chosen, it would be all day and all night, too. Not only does the express for Madrid leave at night, but that from Madrid to San Sebastian, so that we have the prospect before us of two such journeys. A peculiarity of the passenger trains in Spain, and there is the same in France also, is, that a narrow ledge or platform runs all around them, on which the conductor walks while visiting the different cars to examine or collect the tickets. We have always thought it dangerous and felt afraid of some accident, and our apprehensions were verified in going from Grenada to Algeciras. The

train stopped suddenly in the open country. There was at once a great excitement among the passengers, who could
not imagine what had happened, but presently we were told the conductor had
fallen off and had struck on his head.
Fortunately he was not seriously hurt, and
after a delay of a quarter of an hour we
started again. It was suggested by some
one that perhaps the reason why the trains
in Spain go so slowly is that the conduct-
ors may escape being killed when they
fall off. This arrangement, like many
others over here, would not suit our
people very well.

DEAR ——.

We have now reached the northern
boundary, and when we quit this pretty
watering-place our Spanish trip will be
over. We stayed in Seville to witness
the ceremonies of Corpus Christi, and
then went on to Madrid. We were much
pleased with the curious dance that we
saw in the cathedral on the morning of

the great feast, a performance that takes place nowhere in the world but in Seville. The consecrated host was exposed upon the altar, and ten boys danced before it for nearly half an hour. The boys were beautifully dressed and had castanets, which they used at intervals. The dance was a slow one, of the nature of a minuet, and the boys sang, as they danced, the same air that was played by the orchestra. The procession, which began immediately after the dance, though very fine in some respects, was a little disappointing. There was a great display of silver and embroideries and fine vestments, but it did not seem so imposing as the simple processions we have at home, when the priest carries through the church the Blessed Sacrament, and little girls dressed as angels strew flowers in its path, while the altar boys immediately precede it, constantly throwing incense from their censers. The eve of Corpus Christi the city was beautifully illuminated. As is the case at all Spanish festivals, women were

cooking and selling in the streets buñue-
los, a kind of doughnut fried in fat, which
they kept hot by means of little furnaces.
There was an immense crowd walking
about, but every one seemed good-natured
and disposed to be well behaved. We
were obliged to admit that so great a
throng of people in the streets at home
would not have been so orderly. Late in
the afternoon of Corpus Christi we left for
Madrid, which we reached about ten the
next morning. All the Spanish cities we
had hitherto seen had been more or less
of the same type, and all possessed the
national characteristics, but we found, to
our surprise, Madrid entirely different.
The streets are as remarkably wide as
those of the other cities are narrow.
There are statues and fountains and gardens galore, but there is nothing distinctive
about it. It might be Paris or New York
or Berlin, or any of the modern cities of
the world. It is very handsome, but did
not interest us greatly. We like narrow
streets and antique houses, and ruins and

all the signs of age. As soon as possible we visited the famous picture gallery so renowned for its paintings by Murillo and Velasquez. There are also several Raphaels and Andrea del Sartos, and a large number of Riberas. This gallery we found the greatest place of attraction in Madrid, but the Armory proved also extremely interesting. It is probably the finest collection of armor of different styles and epochs in the world. We saw several complete suits that were worn by Charles the Fifth, some that were made for Philip the Second and his son Don Carlos, one that was made for Don John of Austria, and a number worn by Philip the Fourth. We saw also the sword of Isabella the Catholic. Why she had a sword, we do not know, but there it was before our eyes; so we were obliged to believe it. We drove one afternoon in the beautiful park called "El Retiro," and, before entering it, we saw the Queen with the little King, who were on their way to the church that they visit every Saturday afternoon. The open carriage in which they sat had outriders, and in addition was preceded and followed by a number of mounted soldiers in gay uniforms. The Queen was tastefully dressed in a lilac bonnet and lilac silk dress or wrap. She has never worn any color but black or white or purple since her husband's death. The little King, who is eight years old and a delicate-looking child, was dressed mostly in white, with a wide-brimmed white straw hat. We should have known them, I think, even without "all the pomp and circumstance of state" that surrounded them, from seeing their photographs, which are sold in all the book-stores, and are excellent likenesses. I must retract what I said in a former letter about the beauty of Spanish women, so far as Madrid is concerned. We saw a number of very handsome girls while driving, and were impressed with the idea that it was rare to see on such an occasion so great an amount of good looks. We left Madrid on Saturday evening, and stopped at Burgos at five o'clock in the morning, in order to see the great cathedral. We found that it differed from others we have visited in having its massive pillars adorned with statues, skilfully carved out of solid stone. These statues stand out all around the upper portions of the pillars, and have a very curious and beautiful effect. The stonework of the cathedral throughout is wonderful. We should have been better able to enjoy it if it had not been so early in the morning when we saw it, after a partially sleepless night. Its beauty was much interfered with, in our opinion, by having the choir placed in the middle of the church, and entirely preventing the grand effect that one has in great Gothic cathedrals, when standing at the entrance and looking up the nave to the high altar. It is this view which is so magnificent in the Cologne cathedral. There was little else of interest in Burgos, and the hotels are said to be very poor, so, after remaining a few hours, we came on here. But few of the hotels in Spain are really good ;

with the exception of the Hotel de Madrid, in Seville, we did not find one to which we could give anything like unqualified praise. The food and cooking in most of them are poor, according to American ideas. We should sometimes have found it difficult to take enough to satisfy our hunger, had it not been for the oranges which were always on the table at the *déjeûner* and dinner, and which were, as a general thing, delicious. The milk used is usually goat's milk, which is very unpalatable in its natural state, but which, when boiled, answers very well for coffee and for all ordinary cooking purposes. The butter and cheese made from it are not agreeable to the American taste. In some places, however, we succeeded in getting cow's milk. The want of ice makes a great difference in the meat. It has to be cooked so fresh that it is hard and tough. We saw at least one establishment for the manufacturing of artificial ice ; and we were told that it was not dear, so why it does not come into general use we can't imagine, unless it is because the people have become so accustomed to doing without it, they don't desire any change. I have not yet spoken of one important institution in Spain, that of the Guarda Civil. This is a band of picked men taken from the soldiery, and selected on account of their courage and other fine qualities. Some of them were on every train by which we travelled, and they are placed wherever there is need of them throughout the country. We were told that before the establishment of this guard, lawlessness prevailed, and that robberies on the trains were of frequent occurrence. Now that is all changed, and order and good government appear to be found everywhere. The Queen is said to have shown herself a most efficient ruler, and to have finally brought over to her side so eminent an advocate of republicanism as Emilio Castellar. For all that, she is not very popular with the people at large, principally because she is not a Spaniard. I was talking with a Spanish

lady in Barcelona on the subject, and I
said I could not understand why the Queen
was not more popular, if she were so good
a woman and so excellent a ruler. "Why,
you would not like," she replied, "to have
a foreigner, President of the United States,
to rule over you." This certainly was an
"argumentum ad feminam," and for a
moment I was silenced, but, after a little
reflection, I told her that I did not believe
I should mind it, provided he were de-
voted to republican principles and to the
true interests of our country. The Queen
and her son have certainly a noble dwel-
ling place. The Royal Palace at Madrid
is said to be the finest kingly residence in
Europe. We could not go over it, because it is only exhibited to strangers
when the Queen is not there; but we
stood in the great square in front and
looked down upon the beautiful view of
the valley lying before us and the Guada-
marra mountains in the distance. As to
whether the palace is the finest in Europe,
there may be some difference of opinion,

but there can be little doubt that few have such a panorama of loveliness stretched out before the gaze of their inhabitants. The Queen in summer comes here to San Sebastian, where she has a villa, and of which she is said to be very fond. It is a romantic, rock-bound coast, a little in the style of Newport, with a short stretch of beach, where the bathers disport themselves. We start soon for the frontier on our way to Lourdes, and so good-bye to old Spain, which, in spite of all its drawbacks, its bull-fights, its want of education among the inhabitants, and the low rank it takes among the nations, is to many a land of enchantment and delight.

NORWAY

BALHOLM, SOGNEFIORD, NORWAY, July 20, 1894.

DEAR ——.

One week ago, to-day, we began our travels in this land of lakes, fiords, and mountains, of glaciers and avalanches. We first came over from England, crossing in the steamer El Dorado from Hull to Stavanger, and a week ago we began our present trip from Stavanger in the south to Molde in the north—a journey which includes most of the finest scenery of Norway—by going through the fiord on which Stavanger is situated to Sand. There we took one of the vehicles of the country, the stohlkjaerre with a fine Norwegian pony, and were driven by a small boy to Oosen on the Sudal lake. Oosen is a small place, containing only a few houses, two of which are rustic hotels. We chose the more attractive-looking one of the two, but found our entertainment of a most primitive character. We could not obtain any supper until nine o'clock, and then found the "pièce de resistance" to be reindeer, which some of our party did not incline to eat. The bread was very poor, the tea and coffee, ditto, but with some crackers and poached eggs, we managed to make a meal. What was lacking in creature comforts was compensated for by picturesque surroundings. Directly opposite our lodging place, euphemistically termed a hotel, a cliff rose precipitously from the lake to the height of ten or twelve hundred feet. It presented a sheer, straight wall of rock, just such, was remarked by one of the party, as would have suited a South Sea Islander for one of his famous leaps. The water below was of a deep blue, and of the extreme clearness which characterizes most of the lakes and mountain streams in Norway. I cannot imagine anything more pellucid than this beautiful water; there is not a suspicion of mud or dirt connected with it, and in its purity and loveliness it seems to me emblematic of the character of the people which strikes us as abounding in charming qualities. They have not yet been contaminated by coming into contact with the outside world, but whether this will long be the case, with such an influx of tourists, as is now taking place, appears rather doubtful. We have seen but one beggar since entering Norway, and the relief is great to those who have been afflicted as we have in Italy and Spain and Morocco with a legion of mendicants.

Leaving Oosen the next morning, we went in a little steamer through the beautiful Sudal lake to Naes, where we took our dinner, and there hiring a vehicle, we proceeded through the wonderful Bratlands dal or valley to Horre. There are no railroads anywhere in this part of the country with the exception of one from Vosswanger to Bergen, so there is no way of travelling except by boats when on the water and carriages on land. These latter are of three kinds,—the landau drawn by two horses and the stohlkjaerre and cariole by one. The cariole is a peculiar vehicle, consisting of one small seat and a long narrow stretch of board for the legs of the occupant, which are extended longitudinally and protected by a slightly raised piece of wood in front. In both this and the stohlkjaerre the driver sits or stands behind, unless the passenger chooses to drive himself. The stohlkjaerre is somewhat similar to the cariole, except that it has a seat wide enough for two persons, and a place in front, like ordinary vehicles, for the feet. The landau is the same as a landau everywhere, with a top that can be drawn up or let down at will. In all of these carriages there is a small space behind for light baggage, but not for trunks. Very few persons travel with trunks, but those who do, are obliged to have an extra cart or wagon in which to carry them, as their extra weight would be too much for the stout little ponies when ascending the hills. Although it was raining when we entered the Bratlands dal, as it had been doing most of the time since we arrived in Norway, the beauty of the scenery rendered us insensible to all considerations of discomfort. We were lost in admiration at what we saw around us,—a narrow gorge with high cliffs on either side, rising sometimes to an astonishing height, a mountain torrent rushing through it with an almost deafening roar, foaming and boiling, so that sometimes for a quarter of a mile we could see nothing but spray and foam, except when on the edge it ran a little more quietly, flowing into pools and shallows, and giving us an opportunity to see its exquisite emerald green color. At times it was nearly on a level with the road, at others so far beneath it as to be almost out of sight, the precipitous wall of the chasm on the other side from the road rising higher and higher than before, and increasing, if that were possible, the sublimity of the view. I have been in the Bernese Oberland, and over the St. Gothard pass, as well as in the Tyrol and in some of the finest scenery of the Rocky

Mountains, but I was never more impressed, I think, than by this charming valley.

Upon arriving at Horre, or Breifond, as it is sometimes called, we found the hotel very full, as is generally the case, this being just at the height of the tourist season, but we were so fortunate as finally to secure a room. We were waited upon, as we have been elsewhere, by girls in the native costume,—viz., a white muslin corsage with full sleeves, and over it a red sleeveless jacket, reaching only to the waist, with straps over the shoulders and much ornamented in front. This is worn with a black skirt and usually the addition of a white apron. Most of the Norwegians are fair, with very light hair, so much so, that it is a matter of remark when we see among the waitresses one with dark hair.

Leaving Breifond the next morning, we had a long drive by stohlkjaerre to Odde, on the Hardanger fiord, where we arrived about the middle of the afternoon. Our

way at first led over the Horrebraekker
pass, and to reach it we were obliged to
ascend a mountain so high that, by the
time we reached the top, we found ourselves surrounded by snow. The gentlemen of our party walked up the mountain, the ladies accompanying them a portion of the distance, but were unable to
make the whole ascent on foot. It was
while walking up this mountain that we
made our first acquaintance with the
lemming, an animal peculiar to the Scandi-
navian peninsula. A little creature suddenly ran out before us from its hole in
the rocks. We were lost in astonishment,
never having seen the like before. It
partook of the characteristics of the
guinea-pig, the ground squirrel, and the
mole, and yet was not either. It was very
small, with four short legs, and a mere
apology for a tail, covered with brown
fur except on the back, where it was beautifully marked with white and brown alter-
nating. It ran rapidly, and soon hid itself
behind a stone. We have seen numbers

of them since then, and have learned that they abound in Norway. They are graminivorous, feeding mostly on seeds and roots. The reindeer is perhaps their greatest enemy, often killing them, not for their flesh, but for the vegetable matter in their stomachs. They have a singular habit, it is said, of sometimes collecting together in herds and travelling towards the west; when reaching a river, they swim across it. Finally, they arrive at the sea, when, not knowing apparently the difference, they plunge into it, and after swimming for some time are drowned.

The road over the Horrebraekker pass had just been cleared of snow everywhere except in one place, where we were all obliged to get out of the carriages and walk over the frozen surface. The scenery, though so different from that of the day before, had its own peculiar charm. The snow, in many places five and six feet deep, had begun to thaw under the influence of a summer sun, and everywhere streams of the purest, clearest water were flowing down the hills. In one spot, where there was a hollow among the mountains, they had formed a lake of the same beautiful green color that characterizes the mountain streams. Descending finally into the valley, we stopped at Odde, where we remained over Sunday. On the way, we stopped to see the Laate foss, an unusually fine waterfall, which we admired more than any we have seen. It is in several tiers, there being one descent above another, and it finally divides and ends in two cascades of a magnificent height, separated from each other by a huge rock.

Odde is a great tourist centre, and, being at the head of the Sör fiord, there is a constant communication by steamer between it and Bergen. It has a pretty little church, to which scarcely any one went the Sunday we were there. It is the custom of the surrounding country for the people to attend this church in their native costume once in three weeks. The married women wear a peculiar white cap or head-dress, made with a border, into which a stiffener is introduced so as to make it stand out all around the face. It then descends in the back in several stiff rolls nearly to the waist. We regretted greatly that the Sunday we were there did not happen to be the right one to give us an opportunity to see them. There are two favorite excursions from Odde,—one to the Buar brae, a glacier which is an offshoot from the Folgefond, and the other to a water-fall called the Skaegedals foss, which is one of the largest in Europe, but which several who had been there told us they did not admire so much as the Laate foss. I must explain that "foss" is the Norwegian word for cataract, "brae" for glacier, "dal" for valley, and "vaud" for water or lake.

Upon leaving Odde, we drove to Vossewangen, where we took the train for Bergen. This is the only railroad in the western part of Norway, and is a model of engineering skill. It is only seventy miles long, but cost an immense amount of money on account of the difficulty of cutting through the mountains nearly every foot of the way. Short as it is, it has fifty-five tunnels. It took us about three hours to reach Bergen. Upon arriving, we went to Holt's Hotel, which is considered the best in the city, and is pleasantly situated near the public park, where a fine band plays every evening in summer from nine o'clock until eleven. It seems strange that it should begin at such an hour and continue so late, but everything in Norway, so far as the evenings are concerned, is late, which we attribute to the extreme length of the days, causing nine o'clock to seem as seven does in our country. Dinner is usually in the middle of the day and supper at eight or half-past eight o'clock. This would be very inconvenient were there places of entertainment to be attended in the evenings, but there did not appear to be any.

We stayed a day and a half in Bergen,

and found it an interesting city, very picturesquely situated. We were particularly charmed with the street called the Torv Almenigen or Market Square. It is short and extremely wide, with the markets occupying the lower portion of it, and at either end a background of mountains rising up in silent majesty like sentinels guarding the city. A statue to a prominent Norwegian named Christie ornaments the centre of this interesting street. There are a good many fine shops both here and in the Strand Gade, containing a great variety of articles of the celebrated Norwegian silver work, and other industries of the country. We visited the picture-gallery, but it is not one of remarkable merit. Upon leaving Bergen we returned to Vossewangen, and there took a carriage for Stalheim. This time we had a landau with two horses; but it did not seem to be any easier for them to draw two persons (our party was for the nonce reduced to two) than it has been for the little Nor-

wegian pony that we usually have. This
breed of ponies is remarkable. They
appear to possess great strength and en-
durance, climbing hills like a cat, and
always sure-footed and reliable. They
are mostly of a light roan or cream color.
They are accustomed to walk slowly up
hill, but they make the descent of all except the very highest with the greatest
rapidity. The manner in which they
dash down the hills makes me hold my
breath, and reminds me of stories I have
heard of the way in which the old stage-
coaches were driven. Nothing but coast-
ing or tobogganing can compare with it.
These charming ponies are fat and in
good condition in every respect, and seem
to be very well treated by their drivers,
a whip being scarcely ever used upon
them. They are driven generally by
boys, but sometimes by men, and occasionally by women or little girls. It
seemed very strange to us the first time
we saw a little maiden of eleven or twelve
years of age get up behind a cariole to

conduct a gentleman on the next stage of his journey.

We reached the hotel at Stalheim in the middle of the afternoon and remained until the next morning. This is one of the most celebrated places in Norway, and nothing that we have seen, except the Bratland's dal, has pleased us so much. Situated on a mountain, surrounded by sister peaks rearing their heads still higher towards the heavens and looking down upon the Eredal, the hotel commands a magnificent view. As we approached it, the Eredal appeared to be a mere gorge or opening in the mountains, but upon coming nearer we could see that it was a splendid valley, narrow throughout its whole extent and gradually growing wilder and more sombre, but at Stalheim of sufficient width to allow of the cultivation of a number of fields bearing the usual crops of oats, barley, and potatoes. Nothing else except grass will apparently do well in these latitudes. The climate is too cold for wheat, and there does not seem to be an attempt on the part of any one to have a vegetable garden. There is, consequently, a great deficiency in this important part of the cuisine. We have constantly the finest fish—salmon and trout as well as other varieties—in great abundance, a moderate supply of meat, that placed before us being sometimes beef, sometimes reindeer or kid, as the case may be, but no vegetables of any account beside potatoes, and very little fruit.

Leaving Stalheim the next morning, we walked down the mountain, the result being an attack of lameness on the part of one of us, from the excessive use of muscles unaccustomed to such exertion, and then drove through the magnificent Eredal to Gutwangen, where we took the steamer on the Sognefiord for this place, —Balholm,—beautifully situated near the head of one of the arms of the fiord. The air is very mild here, the fiord a charming place for water excursions, so that it is a very popular spot with the English,

some of whom come to reside during the
summer. After our arrival, about three
o'clock in the afternoon, we hired a row-
boat, and spent an hour and a half on the
fiord in a most enjoyable manner. From
Balholm it is customary to go into the
Fierland fiord, another arm of the bay,
and make an excursion to the Jostedal
brae, the largest glacier in Europe. It
covers an immense area of ground, and
extends its branches in twenty-four points
down towards the level of the lakes and
fiords. Those who are not strong enough
to climb to its summit to view it in all its
glory, can have their vision gladdened,
when sailing on the neighboring waters,
by a sight of these immense spectral arms
lighting up the landscape with their glit-
tering white surfaces, while on near in-
spection the great mass of ice is found to
be of a beautiful blue color. Balholm is
such a charming spot, we were loath to
leave it; but the length of the trip we had
yet to make did not allow us to linger
there any longer.

HELLESILT, July 24, 1894.

DEAR ———.

We arrived last evening at this little village on the Nord fiord, after a day of hard travel, including a sail of several hours in the morning on the Nord fiord, and the whole of the rest of the day, except when we stopped to get our dinner, in driving on the road. It was rather fatiguing, but not enough so to prevent our enjoying a good night's rest after it.

Upon leaving Balholm we went in the steamer on the Sognefiord to Vadheim, and there we took stohlkjaerres for Förde. It was a long drive, and nearly the whole of it in a hard rain. Every day since we came to Norway it has rained more or less, generally more, until to-day. So much wet weather has interfered considerably with our comfort, being out of doors so much as we have been, from morning till night; but if, instead of rain, we had been troubled with dust, it might have been even more disagreeable. We had a remarkably fine horse—one, as we suppose, of the celebrated Förde breed—in our stohlkjaerre, and we dashed down the hills faster than ever before. When we reached the hotel at Förde in a very moist condition, we were greeted by two young men of our acquaintances, two Americans, who were travelling together, and who had preceded us by a few hours. They had left Vadheim the afternoon before and had gone as far as Sande, where they spent the night. They told us of an adventure they had on the way, which came near ending seriously. They had only gone a short distance from Vadheim, when they perceived a boulder, which had come down from the mountains and fallen or rolled directly into the middle of the road. The roads in Norway are narrow at best, bordered on one side or both, instead of a fence, with large granite stones, set three or four feet apart, as protection against accident. In this case the road on one side was at the foot of the mountains, and on the other was on the

edge of an embankment or cliff, where
there was a descent of about twenty-five
or thirty feet to the ground below. When
our friends found their way stopped by the
great stone or boulder, they were in doubt
what course to pursue. It was entirely too
heavy to be rolled aside, so they had to
devise some other plan. They got out of
their stohlkjaerre and decided that they
would get the driver to lead the horse
around the boulder, while they held up the
two outside wheels of their vehicle, which
hung over the cliff in mid-air, and so they
thought they would conquer the difficulty.
But they reckoned without their host in
supposing they could do so, for, in the
attempt, one of the wheels on the inside
struck the boulder, and in an instant the
horse and carriage went down the thirty
feet,—the men, however, escaping. They
feared the horse was killed or seriously
injured, but in a little while he appeared
to have recovered from the shock, and to
be as well as ever. They had an hour
of hard work before they could get their

stohlkjaerre up the bank, and they arrived
at Sande about midnight.

We stayed only one night at Förde, and
the next morning drove to Nedre Vasen-
den, where we took a little steamer and
went on the picturesque Jelstervaud to
Skei or Skej, as it is sometimes spelled.
We were troubled, as usual, with rain,
which kept coming in upon us, although
our boat had an awning, so that we were
not sorry to disembark at Skei and remain
until the next day. As that was Sunday,
we concluded to take a little rest, and did
not leave until the afternoon. This gave
us an opportunity to see the peasantry
driving by to their church, which was at a
little distance from the hotel, for morning
service. The native costume which they
wore was quite different from that at Odde.
There the married women had stiff white
caps, which set out from the head like an
aureole and descended in several pieces
behind nearly to the waist. Here they
wore peaked black velvet or stuff caps,
which stood up some distance above their

heads like a bishop's mitre, and were finished with a ruche where they came close to their faces. The unmarried girls in both places seemed to prefer dark-colored handkerchiefs of some cotton material tied over their heads. The dress of a bride is very singular in this part of Norway. She wears a metal crown on her head and numerous ornaments, including sometimes a looking-glass, on her breast.

Some of the customs of the people are peculiar, one of the most so, that of shaking hands with a person who gives them anything or does them a favor. We are many times a day called upon to go through with this ceremony with the drivers of our stohlkjaerres, or the boatmen who have rowed us on the lakes. It wounds their feelings extremely if any one refuses to grasp their proffered hand, and we are very careful to respond always cordially to their advances. We often wish they knew a little more English than they do. The little they can say is spoken with such an excellent pronunciation and accent that it is very misleading. Every day we flatter ourselves that we have secured a driver with whom we can have some conversation. He will say, for example, "How far do you want to go?" or, "This is a good horse," alluding to the merits of the steed he wishes us to engage, almost as well and with as little foreign accent as we could utter it. At once we are delighted,—for we never learn by previous experience,—and think that now we have found a treasure. Then some such conversation as this will occur. As we come to a lake, we say, "Driver, what is the name of this lake?"

"Lake, yes."

"But I did not ask you if it was a lake. I could see that myself. I asked you its name?"

"Don't understand."

Presently we begin again. "Driver, are there any bears in these mountains?"

"Mountains, yes."

"But, driver, what we asked you is, are there are any bears, bears (baaren, for we invariably fall into German when we are desperate, with a conviction that it must make the matter clear to them) in these mountains ?"

" Don't understand."

So it is with everything. Sometimes, instead of saying that they " don't understand," they take refuge in silence, and reply not a word. We have determined to learn some Norwegian phrases, so that we shall not be so utterly nonplussed ; but we are beginning rather late, I fear, to improve our knowledge of Norsk, as they call it. Although the pronunciation of English is, as we have said, so remarkably good here, the people seem to have a difficulty in learning the language perfectly. Even those who profess to know it well enough to write advertisements are not proficient, as is evident from some of the notices posted around in the different places. In this hotel there is one in the second story hall, telling what should be done by the guests in case of fire. It concludes by saying that they will find a stair-

case at the end of the house which leads
on to the "hig-way," meaning, of course,
highway.   Another that we have heard of
says that a certain house for the entertainment of guests is most conveniently situated for the " see-worthy" mountains in
the neighborhood.   In the hotel where
we stopped in Bergen, the following was
posted on the wall in every room : " Trav-
ellers are requested, in order to safe
guard the mutual comfort, not to indulge
in vociferous language after twelve o'clock
at night."   "Vociferous language," we
thought good, and we wondered what
sort of guests they were in the habit of
having, it being the first hotel in Bergen.

On Sunday afternoon, we left the friends
who had been travelling with us for several days at Skei and went in a stohlkjaerre to Sandene, on the Nord fiord.
The ordinary way of continuing the journey to Molde, a point of great interest,
is to drive to Utvik on the same fiord,
and afterwards cross over to Faleide.   As
the road, however is very hilly between

Egge and Utvik, we decided, after reaching Egge, to make a little detour and go by the way of Red and Sandene, which would insure us a comfortable drive. We were very glad that we did so, as it afforded us an opportunity of seeing a most beautiful lake in the neighborhood of Sandene, called Bradheim's vaud. The road, which for some distance ran along a height above the lake, was so finely made that it was in itself an object of interest. The rocks which towered above our heads were of the finest granite, and bore everywhere the marks of the blasting that had been necessary in order to build the road. The lake itself, however, proved the greatest attraction, not so much on account of its surroundings, which are not so striking as those of many others, but from the exquisite light-green color of the water, for which we could not at first account, as it was different from anything we had ever seen before in any part of the world. We found, upon regarding it more closely, that the supply of the lake was largely due to a river running into it of the same peculiar light-green, and came to the conclusion that the color of the river was caused by the whitish, milk-like water, such as comes from a glacier mixing with the usual blue of the mountain streams. Owing to the cause, whatever it was, the lake was not so transparent as others we have seen, but this was more than compensated by the unchanging beauty of its color. In the other lakes and fiords on which we have sailed the appearance changes, owing to the presence or absence of sunlight, and they are sometimes of an attractive color, at other times gray and dull-looking; but the water in Bredheim's vaud was unvaryingly beautiful. We enjoyed the drive very much in spite of our usual attendant, the rain, and reached Sandene in time for supper. Yesterday morning we took a steamer on the fiord as far as Faleide, and from there, as I have said, had a long drive, changing horses several times to this place, Hellesilt, on the same fiord. The lemmings seem to be unusually abundant in this neighborhood, and as we were nearing this village we saw them constantly running across the road a little ahead of our carriage. They have apparently so little fear of man it speaks well for the humanity of the Norwegians. All these stopping-points of our journey are set down on the map in such a manner as to make them seem of considerable importance; and we are always amazed upon reaching them to find that they consist of from ten to twenty houses, and occasionally can only boast of five or six. If they have ten houses, one of them will be a hotel; if twenty, there will probably be two houses of entertainment. This village is very prettily situated. There is a fine view of the fiord in front, and at the side of the hotel, only a short distance from it, a mountain river dashes down a rocky descent, making an imposing waterfall. We are going to remain here until to-morrow, so as to go this afternoon into the Geiranger, a branch of the Nord fiord, which is said to be remarkably fine. There is a book of photographs of Norwegian scenery in the drawing-room here; but they do not usually attract us in the least, from the fact that they so inadequately depict what they are intended to represent. No photographs can do justice to the subject. Everything in Norway is on so grand a scale that the productions of the camera, fine as many of them are, fall far short of the reality, and consequently we feel that we should prefer to have no representation of beauties that would only be belittled thereby, but trust to our memory to preserve unimpaired the recollection of all the grandeurs we have witnessed.

MOLDE, July 30, 1894.

DEAR ———.

Everywhere that we have been in Norway the farmers have been making hay. The grass was cut about the time we arrived, and ever since they have been trying to dry it, rather a difficult matter it would seem in the districts where we have had so much rain. The manner in which they dry it is to put it on to frames and change it frequently. These frames are made by standing a number of stakes in the ground about three feet apart, and then fastening to them longitudinally other stakes, or sometimes wires, by means of the flexible stems of plants or the long fibres of roots. These frames become so heavy with all the grass hung upon them that they sometimes have to be supported by additional stakes driven into the ground a short distance away, propped against them. Everywhere we go that we see farms of fields under cultivation they are full of these frames. Another thing we often see, and which has interested us very much, is the number of wires reaching from the top of a high cliff or mountain and fastened by a windlass in the valley below near farm-houses, so that grass or hay can be sent down on them, as well as milk, fire-wood, and sometimes other articles. In the early summer the cows are driven up into the mountains to pasture, as is done in Switzerland, and they do not come down again till the autumn is at hand, hence some means is needed of sending their milk to the valleys below. We were very desirous of seeing a can of milk come down over the wire, and one day our wish was gratified. We heard a whizzing noise, and, looking over at a little distance to where a farmhouse stood, we saw the can descending quickly, but not too much so. There is some arrangement acting like a brake which prevents it from coming too fast. The oats are now ripe, and are beginning to be cut and fastened upon long upright sticks to dry. As I have said before, the only crops are oats, barley, hay, and potatoes. Never, even in Southern Norway, did we see anything else. We cannot imagine why more vegetables are not planted. If the climate is too cold for wheat, we should think it possible to raise turnips and onions without any difficulty.

Most of the lighter part of the farm work is done by women, the ploughing of the fields and the cutting of the crops being usually undertaken by the men. We saw about three times as many women as men at work in the fields during the season that we were there.

The farmers seem to be a contented sort of people; indeed, an absence of greed appears a characteristic of the nation. A gentleman whom we have met in travelling said that he had the following conversation with a farmer, one of those occasionally to be seen who speak English. Our friend said to him, "You must make very little money by your farming."

"Yes," was the reply; "but we don't want money."

"Why, you need it for your clothes."

"No; we weave the cloth at home and make our clothes."

"But your hats?"

"Our hats? Why, my wife makes the felt and then the hats."

"Well, you must buy your carts and wagons."

"No; we cut down the trees and get the wood, and make our wagons all at home."

"How about the harness for your horses? you certainly buy that."

"No; we have the hides of our cattle, and make the leather ourselves for our shoes and our harness."

"Well, the bits? you don't make them, do you?"

"No; there we have to use some money. We must buy the iron for our axles and the tires of the wheels as well as for the bits; but in my father's time we used oaken bits, and for my part I think them just as good as the iron ones."

There are a great many little farms, consisting often of only a few fields, on the sides of the mountains and in every spot where it is possible to cultivate the ground. We have been interested to know whether these belong to the men who plough and till the soil, and have found upon inquiry that they do. The land in every case has been in the family for generations, and it is left always to the eldest son, or, where there are no sons, to the eldest daughter, so that the property may be preserved intact.

Before leaving Hillesilt, where my last letter was written, we had the pleasure of visiting the Geiranger fiord, which is one of the wonders of Norway. The fiord is full of tortuous windings, and so narrow that it appears at a little distance as if there could not possibly be room to pass in places where the tremendous cliffs coming down to the water's edge seem to meet each other; yet, upon nearer approach, there is always a slight opening disclosed wide enough for the passage of the steamer. There are several waterfalls, but not of great volume, and they did not impress us nearly so much as the immense height of the cliffs and their peculiar shape. Some of these fiords are in places, it is said, several thousand feet in depth, which fact is calcu-

lated rather to add to the timidity of a ner-
vous person when rowing or sailing over
them. The next day we left Hillesilt,
and succeeded, with some difficulty, in
reaching here about ten o'clock in the
evening. We went in a steamer on the
fiord as far as Söholt, and there we landed
and took stohlkjaerres for Vestnaes on
the other side of the fiord from Molde.
The drive was delightful, particularly so
when the road led along the fiord. Molde
is in a sheltered situation, and, although it
is several degrees north of St. Petersburg,
the vegetation is comparatively luxuriant.
The same can be said of Vestnaes; and
the drive, as we approached it, seemed as
if it might be through a gentleman's park.
The grass and trees were fresh and green,
as they would be with us in May. When
we arrived at Vestnaes, we found that the
little steamer which runs between that
place and Molde would not make another
trip that evening. The hotel-keeper at
Vestnaes would doubtless have been glad
if we had passed the night there, but we

were very anxious to go on to Molde, and resolved to try a row-boat. We secured three rowers and a rather poor, leaky boat with a small sail, as there did not seem to be any better one, and began our trip of eleven miles. The fiord, which was so wide that it seemed almost like the open sea, was in some places very rough, and our trip was a long one. The wind, what there was of it, was dead ahead, so that we had to depend more upon our oars than upon our canvas. We were surprised to find that our men did not understand the management of the sail better. They attempted to steer directly for Molde, which brought the wind dead ahead, and consequently the sail could not help us at all. One of our party, an excellent amateur sailor, remained silent until he could endure it no longer, and then proposed to the men by means of gestures, for they understood no English except a few words, to let him take the helm. As they made no opposition, he seated himself in the middle of the boat, which is where the Norwegians steer, and soon succeeded by his good management in increasing our rate of speed. This want of a thorough knowledge of boat-sailing on the part of our men, which we have had occasion to remark again and again while here at Molde, astonished us the more, as we had seen such superb seamanship on the part of the officers of the steamers on the lakes and fiords. We had a specimen of it on the fiord just after leaving Stavanger on the first day of our trip. The steamers carry the mails, and it is often necessary for them to come up to each other in order to make an exchange of postal matter. We saw a steamer coming, and our boat at once slackened its speed and prepared to go alongside, which it did in the most skilful manner. We could not have believed that it would go so close as it did— within a distance of two or three inches from the other—and yet not touch or even graze it. While an exchange of mails was being effected, a third steamer came alongside of ours in a similarly masterful manner.

Our trip to Molde was a long one in spite of the improved management of the sail, and was a hard pull for the men, there being five passengers in the boat, and yet their price for the whole number was four kroner, a kron being equivalent to our quarter of a dollar.

We thought it was too little, and insisted upon giving them two kroner more, to which they objected, saying it was too much, but they finally accepted it. This incident affords an example of the want of acquisitiveness on the part of the Norwegians, of which I have before spoken. We noticed it in everything relating to money. We began by paying the man or boy or girl, as it might happen to be, who drove our stohlkjaerre, a "pour boire" at least twice as large as that mentioned in the guide-books as the proper sum to pay. There was never any pleasure manifested at this extra consideration, nor did they seem to care whether we gave them the usual amount or twice as much. This entire want of avarice, joined to the truthfulness, honesty, industry, and cleanliness of the Norwegians, has caused us to form the high opinion of the national character which I expressed in my first letter.

Upon arriving at ten o'clock in the evening, we found comfortable quarters at the Alexandra Hotel, and settled ourselves here for the coming week or ten days. Molde is a rather pretty seaside town, the Brighton of Norway. It is beautifully situated on the north side of the Molde fiord, and commands a splendid view of an extensive chain of mountains, among them some of the highest in the Romsdal and other valleys. We spent most of the day after our arrival in walking through the town and making ourselves acquainted with our new surroundings. There are two celebrated excursions from here,—one to the Romsdal and the other to the Eikisdal. As we wished to make them both, we concluded to begin

with the Romsdal, and to start for there
on the next day. The boat which was to
take us to Andalasnaes, the beginning
of the Romsdal, did not leave until three
o'clock in the afternoon. We should like
to have started earlier, in order to get
through the Romsdal to Ormien the same
night, but we were obliged to accommo-
date our movements to those of the boat.
We reached Andalasnaes a little before
eight o'clock, and remained at the hotel
for supper. It was a clear, beautiful night,
and, as we could see the scenery of the
Romsdal to great advantage, we decided
to go through to Ormien the same night.
We knew it would keep us up very late,
but we felt uncertain as to what the
weather might be the next day. More-
over, it is never dark, so that in most respects we can travel as well at night as in
the day. We had with us several friends
who came to the same decision as ourselves, so that we had quite a cavalcade
of carioles and stohlkjaerres making their
way through the Romsdal in the "wee

sma' hours ayont the twal." The tremendous cliffs on each side of the valley frowned down upon us, but did us no harm. They had not always been so considerate, judging from the tremendous boulders that were scattered around on both sides of the road.

One of the most interesting sights in the Romsdal was these immense masses of rock in such numbers and confusion that they seemed as if they might have been playthings thrown about by the Titans of old. Some of them were as large as a four-story house. What a tremendous shock to the earth must have been given when one of these came down from the mountain. An acquaintance of ours told us that on one occasion he witnessed the fall of a comparatively small boulder. As it alighted, it was driven several feet into the earth, then jumped a distance of ten feet in the air, and went rolling along over the ground till it finally settled itself in the position it was to keep for all time.

We did not arrive at Ormien, our stopping-place, until a few minutes before two o'clock, but we found the rustic hotel lighted and some one ready to receive us, which was a great comfort, as we had feared that every one would have retired. We slept during the remainder of the night, and, after an eight o'clock breakfast, returned through the Romsdal to Andalasnaes. The morning was not clear, and the tops of all the mountains were obscured by clouds, so that we were very glad to have seen the famous valley on the preceding evening in a clear and brilliant atmosphere.

We stopped at two stations to rest and feed the horses, and at one of them, called Horgheem, we found the view up the valley particularly beautiful. After dining at Andalasnaes, we went on board the steamer and returned to Molde, reaching here about supper-time.

MOLDE, August 2, 1894.

DEAR ——.

We returned last evening from our
excursion to the Eikisdal, having given
only two days to it, whereas three is the
time usually allotted by tourists. We
found that if we went to Nöste, the village
by which we enter the Eikisdal, and returned the same way, it would certainly
require three days, and we had not so
much time at our disposal, so we resolved
to reach Nöste in another manner,—viz.,
by stohlkjaerre and row-boat, leaving here
on Tuesday morning and returning by the
steamer which leaves Nöste Wednesday
afternoon.   This plan we carried out after
various adventures "by flood and field,"
and saw the Eikisdal satisfactorily. We
left here a little after eight o'clock, and
after a long drive, the first part of which
was very agreeable, as it was along the
Fannestrand,—a beautiful road along the
fiord and the fashionable drive of Molde,
—we reached the village of Tjelde, on the

Lange fiord, about three in the afternoon. At a small station called Eide,—there appear to be several Eides in Norway,— where we stopped some time to rest and feed the horse, we received a most friendly greeting,—not from any member of the human family, but a quadruped in the shape of a fine young heifer. We were seated under the trees in the shade, to escape the heat of the midsummer sun, when this gentle creature advanced toward us and placed her nose against our hands. Acting upon the hint, we rubbed her head and neck, which seemed to give her the greatest pleasure. It was difficult to satisfy her, and we were kept busy stroking her during a considerable portion of our stay. Even after we had discontinued our caresses she would not leave us, but lay down on the grass close to our feet so long as we remained. I never had the same experience elsewhere, and I thought what a striking illustration it afforded of the kindness with which animals are treated in Norway, and which induces affection and a want of timidity on their part. I have never seen horses so well cared for and so much considered anywhere else. They are driven, as a general thing, without either check-rein or blinders; they are scarcely ever struck with the whip, and are so well fed and groomed that it is a pleasure to look at them. There are drinking troughs placed along the roads at intervals, and they are allowed to drink as much and as often as they desire. Having no check-reins they can easily help themselves, and to the grass growing by the wayside whenever they have an opportunity. When going up the hills, of which, as may be supposed, there are a great many, the driver always gets out and walks, and very often the passengers do likewise. The good result of all this care is shown in the amount of work the stout little ponies can do without any apparent injury. They are frequently driven between twenty and thirty miles in one morning or afternoon, but are stopped on the way to be fed and rested. The friendly relations that exist between them and their drivers are most agreeable to witness. When stopping for a momentary halt before going up a steep hill, their drivers often go to them and rub their heads and stroke them, speaking at the same time a few encouraging words.

Upon reaching Tjelde at about three o'clock, we sought a hotel, but could find nothing but a little farm-house, where we succeeded with considerable difficulty in getting, not a dinner, but a simple meal of boiled eggs and bread and milk, with some freshly-picked currants. We then engaged two boatmen to row us over to Nöste, a distance of about eleven miles.

Our party by this time was reduced to two, so that we did not need so many rowers. After much delay, we were settled with our baggage in the ugly, unwieldy boat, but had only gone a short distance when we found that the water was fairly pouring in upon us through the bottom. It came in so fast that it kept one person constantly busy baling it out.

This did not look at all hopeful, nor was it reassuring to timid persons, which, fortunately, we were not. The boatmen themselves seemed shortly to realize that this would not do, and told us by signs—for they could not speak a word of English—that they were going back to the shore to get another boat. This was accomplished, much to our satisfaction, after considerable delay, and then we gave ourselves up to the enjoyment of the eleven-mile row. It was very pleasant at first, but became almost intolerable before we reached Nöste on account of the cramped position in which we were kept. We were rowed out of the Lange fiord, a branch of the great Molde fiord, into another branch, at the end of which Nöste is situated. We found a comfortable hotel there, and took the usual eight o'clock supper. Afterward we had a charming drive with a very spirited pony through a beautiful valley to Overaas, at the end of the Eikisdal-vaud or lake, where we proposed to pass the night. We found lodgings, but of the most primitive character, there being no looking-glass in our room, and the stairs by which we ascended being little better than a ladder. At breakfast we had only steel forks and plated spoons to eat with, but the provender was very good. The situation of Overaas is beautiful in the extreme, and, as we walked out after breakfast, the grandeur of all the surroundings drew from us expressions of the most enthusiastic admiration. We thought, in fact, this entrance to the Eikisdal-vaud more striking than the lake itself, when we came to sail on it. We chartered the little steamer, which is kept to make the round of the lake for the benefit of tourists, and had it all to ourselves. We had heard so much of the Eikisdal-vaud that we were a little disappointed, the reality not equalling our expectations. The Romsdal is the finer excursion of the two, although there are many very attractive points in connection with the Eikisdal.

We finished the tour of the lake at noon, and were able to catch the steamer from Nöste, which brought us back here at a little after eight o'clock. This is our last day in Molde, as to-morrow we start for Bergen, to take passage the next day on the El Dorado back to England.

We have been much gratified at hearing that, from one of the most drunken countries in Europe, Norway has become one of the most sober, and this is attributed mainly to the excellent result of the Gothenberg system. This prevents the tavern- or bar-keepers from making any profit on the sale of alcoholic liquors, so that they have no motive for urging their customers to drink. It affords, however, to the people the greatest facilities for obtaining light wine and beer, care being taken by the government to have all the beer examined to see that it is kept pure and free from alcohol. This excellent beer, which contains probably less alcohol than any other in the world, is drunk in quantities, but has no intoxicating effect, and yet it satisfies the people, so that they seldom seek for stronger beverages. A great desire is felt on the part of some to introduce this system in England, the Bishop of Chester favoring it particularly, as he is an ardent advocate of the Gothenberg method of regulating the liquor traffic, and we hope that the experiment may be tried.

BERGEN, August 4, 1894.

DEAR ——.

We arrived here yesterday about one o'clock, having sailed from Molde at five on the previous afternoon. The sail was a beautiful one, taking us among the numerous islands on the coast of Norway. We never saw anything like it,—islands to the right, to the left, in short, everywhere, some of them inhabited, others nothing but barren rocks. They looked most lovely in the evening light cast by the setting sun, which colored them with a purple sheen and transfigured the whole scene. During the night we passed a boat stranded on one of the islands. We soon ascertained that it was the tourist

steamer Miowera, which left England a
few days before with above a hundred
and fifty passengers. They had only
been out a few days when, through some
mistake of the pilot, she ran upon the
rocks. All the passengers were saved,
and were taken in boats to another
island, where they remained until a passing steamer carried them to Bergen.
When we arrived at our hotel, we found
several of them staying there. The
Canadian Australian company, to which
the Miowera belonged, finally furnished
them with another steamer, and the
greater part of the passengers continued
their journey, the remainder, some of
whom were English and some Americans, giving up the tour and returning to
their respective countries.

This morning we have visited the Han-
seatic Museum, which we missed when
we were here before, and found it most
interesting. It is an exact representation
of one of the houses of the German
merchant princes at the time the Ger-

mans ruled in Norway, and the poor inhabitants of the country were oppressed
in every possible way, not being allowed
to hold any offices or accept any employ-
ment except of a menial kind. These
merchants had under them a foreman and
apprentices, and the latter were treated in
anything but a merciful manner, judging
from the rope's end, knotted and with
nails fastened in it, with which we were
told they were beaten. The merchants,
so long as they remained in Norway,
were not allowed to marry, so that there
should be no mixture with the Norwegians. If they desired to take upon themselves family relations, they were obliged
to return to Germany. They had no fire
in their bedrooms, nor any, apparently, in
their offices, even in winter. In every
"garden," as it is called in Norwegian,
which means court or alley, there was one
general assembling-room for the inhabitants of the different houses, and there
a fire was kept. The beds resembled
bunks, and all opened with doors like

closets in the wall. The only articles of any beauty were the great brazen basin and kettle suspended over it, containing water for toilet purposes.

We leave to-day in the steamer El Dorado for England, looking back upon our sojourn in Norway with much pleasure, and bidding good-by with regret to a country so full of natural beauty and a people so gifted with noble and attractive traits of character.

THE END.